this walker book belongs to:

*In everyone there sleeps
a sense of life lived according to love.*
Philip Larkin

for David Lloyd
J. D.

*for all at Craigmillar
Books for Babies*
P. B.

First published 2009 by Walker Books Ltd
87 Vauxhall Walk, London SE11 5HJ

This edition published 2010

10 9 8 7 6 5 4 3 2 1

Text © 2009 Joyce Dunbar

Illustrations © 2009 Patrick Benson

The right of Joyce Dunbar and Patrick Benson to be identified as
author and illustrator respectively of this work has been asserted by them
in accordance with the Copyright, Designs and Patents Act 1988

This book has been typeset in Gill Sans Schoolbook

Printed in China

British Library Cataloguing in Publication Data:
a catalogue record for this book is available from the British Library

ISBN 978-1-4063-2442-6

www.walker.co.uk

oddly

joyce dunbar

illustrated by

patrick benson

WALKER BOOKS
AND SUBSIDIARIES
LONDON · BOSTON · SYDNEY · AUCKLAND

Round and round in circles went the Lostlet.
"Where am I? Where am I? Where am I?" he sighed.
He twirled a big golden leaf in his hand.
"What I hope… What I hope… What I hope…"
But he didn't know what he was hoping for
so he fell silent.

In and out of shadows skipped the Strangelet.
"What am I? What am I? What am I?" he murmured.
He held a smooth white pebble in his hand.
"What I dream… What I dream… What I dream…"
But he didn't know what he was dreaming of
so he went quiet.

Dancing in the wavelets went the Oddlet.
"Who am I? Who am I? Who am I?" he whispered.
He listened to the pink shell at his ear.
"What I wish… What I wish… What I wish…"
But he didn't know what he was wishing for
so he stopped still.

Running down the road came the little boy.
"Where am I? What am I? Who am I?" he cried.

The Lostlet
stopped in his tracks.

The Strangelet
blinked with surprise.

The Oddlet
flipped right over.

What was this? Who was this?

How did he come to be here?

Stranger, odder, more lost than they.

A boy. Never in their lost, strange, odd little worlds had they ever seen a boy.

The little boy sat down and cried.
The Lostlet ran up to him.
"Hush!" he murmured.
The Strangelet sat beside him.
"Shush!" he whispered.
The Oddlet peered up at the boy.
"What's that noise you are making?" he asked.

"I'm lost," said the boy.
"I ran away so far
  that I can't find my way home."

"Home?" said the Lostlet. "What means home?"
"Home is where I live," said the boy.

"Live?" said the Strangelet. "What means live?"
"I want my Mum," sniffed the boy.

"Mum?" said the Oddlet. "What means Mum?"
The boy cried louder than ever.
"I want some love," he sobbed.

"Love? What means love?" said the Strangelet.

"Can you hold it?" asked the Strangelet.
"Can you twirl it?" asked the Lostlet.
"Can you hear it?" asked the Oddlet.

The little boy stopped crying.

He twirled the golden leaf.

He held the white pebble.

He put the pink shell to his ear.

To the Oddlet he gave a hug.

The Oddlet went very pink.

"So that's what I've been wishing for," he said.

"I'm a Huglet!"

He took the Lostlet by the hand.
The Lostlet gave a shy smile.
"So that's what I've been hoping for," he said.
"I'm a Foundlet!"

they **were** home ...

just in time for supper.

Other books by Joyce Dunbar

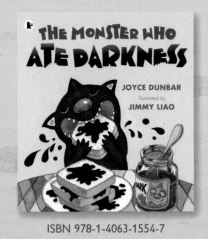

ISBN 978-1-4063-1554-7

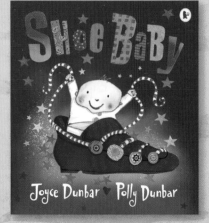

ISBN 978-1-4063-0161-8

Also by Patrick Benson

ISBN 978-1-4063-1335-2

ISBN 978-0-7445-3167-1

Available from all good bookstores

www.walker.co.uk